A WORLD FULL OF
MONSTERS

To my wife, Dorothy, and our sons, John Troy, Jr.,
Gregory Lamont, Garrick Desmond, and Jackson Kinte.

J. T. M.

With love for Jonathon, Katherine, and Hayley—
all of whom are monsters only part of the time.

M. B.

Library of Congress Cataloging-in-Publication Data
McQueen, John Troy.
A world full of monsters.

Summary: A little boy explains away the noises of the
night by telling himself a story about a world full of
friendly monsters.
[1. Monsters—Fiction. 2. Fear—Fiction.
3. Night—Fiction] I. Brown, Marc Tolon, ill.
II. Title.
PZ7.M478825Wo. 1986   [E]   85-48257
ISBN 0-690-04545-X
ISBN 0-690-04546-8 (lib. bdg.)

1 2 3 4 5 6 7 8 9 10
First Edition

John Troy McQueen

A WORLD FULL OF
MONSTERS

illustrated by Marc Brown

Thomas Y. Crowell

New York

A long time ago,

when my grandparents' grandparents
were growing up,
monsters were everywhere.

There weren't any electric lights.

There weren't any cars.

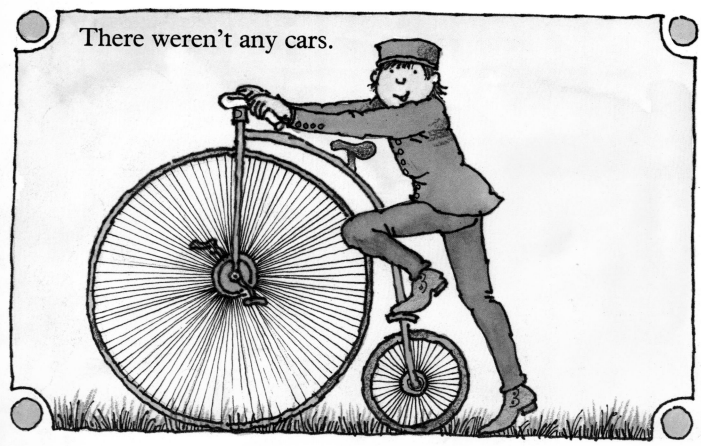

There weren't many big machines.

But there were monsters.

There were monsters in the city.

There were monsters in the country.

In the city monsters were policemen.

The mayor was a monster.

Monsters carried garbage to the city dump.

Monsters put out fires.

Monsters were everywhere you looked.
When you saw one, you just said,
"Hi, Monster," and kept on walking.

In the country, monsters ran the farms.
Monsters cut the hay...

monsters milked the cows...

monsters fed the pigs...

monsters fed the chickens.

Monsters were everywhere you looked.

Monsters played football.

Monsters went bowling.

Monsters played baseball.

Monsters even played tennis.

Monsters were everywhere.

There aren't many monsters left nowadays....

But at night when I hear the
screech, screech, screech sound...

the tick, tick, tick sound…

the scratch, scratch, scratch sound…

the squeak, squeak, squeak sound...

or the drip, drip, drip sound,
I know that it's the sound
of monsters.

When one comes into my room,
I'll just say, "Hi, Monster!"

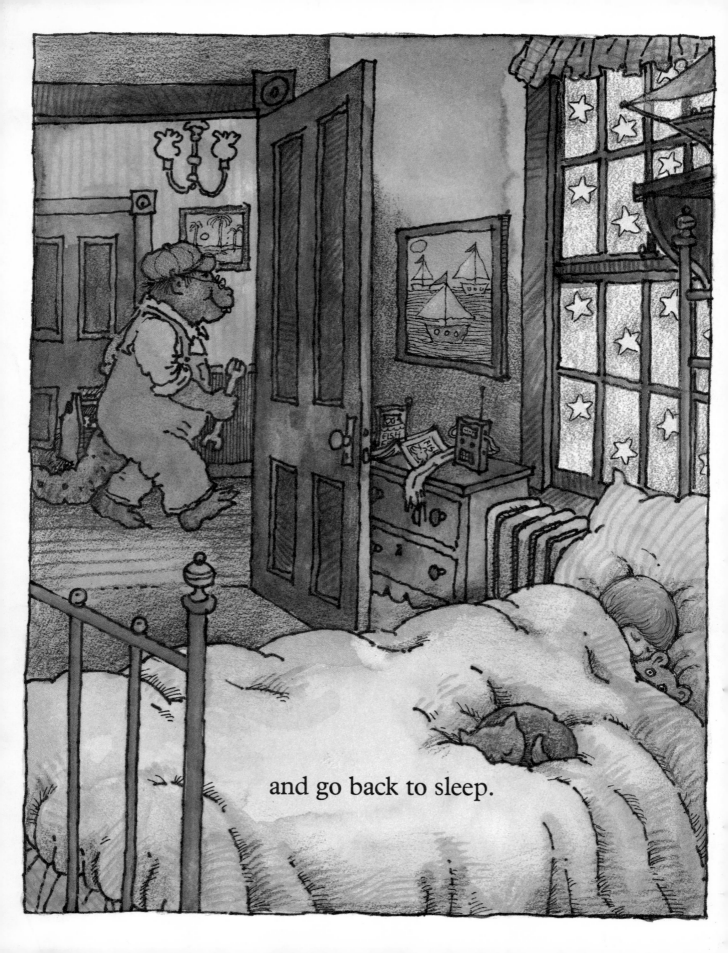

and go back to sleep.